The Prince
and
The Woodcutter

Henry Wolff

With Illustrations by
John Blanche

Paper Tiger

A Dragon's World Ltd., Imprint.
The Bower,
High Street, Limpsfield,
Surrey RH8 0DY,
Great Britain

Distributed by
Phin Ltd.,
Phin House, Bath Road,
Cheltenham, Gloucestershire,
Great Britain.

Produced by M. Dean and S. Henderson.

Setting by Apex Photosetting
Printed in England
ISBN Hardback 0 905895 41 X
ISBN Limpback 0 905895 40 1

For Jenny—sometimes
And Nancy—now

"I dewyne, fordolked of luf-daungere
Of þat pryuy perle wythouten spot."
                                        Pearl

"I want the one rapture of an inspiration,"
                                        G. M. Hopkins

"So lie there now, lie there and
let it be dark, and let the dam break.
Lie there and let the zeroes zing into
you...let them, let it be smashed..."
                                        Stephen Seley

CHAPTER
I

CHAPTER
I:I

There was a time once when a wood-cutter lived on his own in a hut by a stream in a forest. His name was Wyeth. He was known not for felling wood alone but for being honest.

For, if a stiff quarrel outbroke Wyeth was called on to quell it. He would air all sides. Fairly decide. Then give out the truth.

Nor did the woodman waver once. So his name grew, and fame. In time he came to be acclaimed, Wyeth, **The Honest Woodcutter.**

One fine day Wyeth was away in the forest. A stand of pitch-pine swayed to hand. He picked the thickest and best of the lot and got set to chop.

Steady he stood, good and ready to wallop the wood. When then his eyeballs all-but popped.

For, there carved out of bark and root was etched the fetching face of a youth!

The woodman set his axe down.

Amazed, he gazed at the vivid visage, seemed the more he stared more vivid.

He noted the swirls of curls twirl down. The noble nose. The comely chin. The thin, beguiling profile smiling.

Rapt, he blinked at the inky eyes, which, he fancied, blinked back!

Wyeth went weak at the knees.

He drew a breath. His axe he seized. About he wheeled on a heel, to peer at the face from further afield.

Whereat the woodman, taken aback, froze flatfooted in his tracks.

For what he heard was sobs or laughter: then his name came throbbing after....

Where woods thinned fast to wind-worn pasture, a feisty farmer was carting a load of corn to market.

"Hoa!" cried he, seeing the woodman edge from a hedgerow.

Wyeth nodded vaguely.

"Like a lift?"

The woodman freely agreed. He benched at once beside the farmer, who flogged his horses on.

Next they jogged a stretch in silence. Then the woodman, turning earnestly to the farmer, described the forest face.

The farmer was floored.

"Crops!" he cried. "It's got to mean a top-notch year for crops!"

The farmer grinned. His jaw-bones cracked. In the bins of his brain he racked up sack on sack of gain.

"Perhaps," said Wyeth, tactfully.

"Sure as rain!" The other exclaimed.

"So straight to the Royal Square we'll go! There we'll lay this rare affair direct before the King!"

Just then the horses, snorting, stopped. Ahead the road was blocked by flocks of knock-kneed footmen bearing boxes.

What's more, on padded poles they bore a chair enrolled with cloth of gold.

A big *B* was embroidered on it.

"Gangway!" brayed the farmer. "We've got business with the King!"

"Business — !"

Down rolled the cloth of gold. Bold fingers clutched the folds. Then a bald dome shone. Next a set of eyes, and ears.

"What sort of business? I'm a banker, and business is my business!"

A porky face in full pulled clear.

"String along and we'll fill you in! There's no time to lose!"

The farmer's horses clicked their stiff shoes.

"On the double!" The banker bubbled. "Timed saved is money made!"

The banker grinned, through three thick chins.

The footmen flanked the farmer's cart. The banker's chair was cranked in air. Up they started and, as they rode the pot-holed road, Wyeth retold his story.

The banker was bowled over.

"A boon!" He boomed. "Why, sure it means I'll make tycoon!"

His eyeballs rolled. His pink tongue lolled. His fingers told fat sacks of gold.

"Crops it means!" The farmer steamed. "Riches, sir!"

"Crops!"
"Riches!"
"Crops!"
"Riches!"
"Crops! Crops!"
"Gold — !"

The banker glared at the farmer, glared at the banker, back to farmer back to banker back to farmer, forth and back.

At length the glares gave way to stares. In time a standoff was declared.

Again the banker's sly eyes gleamed.

Again the wily farmer beamed.

Both dreamed of booty to be....

Hey — ! "What's the rush?"

The banker blanched, and looked askance.

And there he saw a knight in armour, handsome on a prancing charger.

Daggers dangled at his hips. Gauntlets by the belt were clipped. A lance and sword of fine toledo lay astraddle his soaped saddle.

He was quite a knight.

"We're on our way to see the King! There's precious piddling time to spare!"

The banker rent his absent hair.

"What about?"

"A sign!" The farmer spat, and flat.

"A most valuable sign! We've not a moment more to waste!"

The banker's backside slapped in haste.

"What kind of sign?" the knight asked nicely, now riding abreast.

The farmer moaned.

The banker groaned.

The pair stared at Wyeth who, to the knight's polite petition, swiftly outlined the position.

The knight went white with excitement.

"Cripes!" He piped. "It doubtless means I'll take the tourney!"

His eyes came clear. His stallion reared. His eardrums hummed with cheers to come.

"Gold!" The boiling banker howled.

"Crops!" The spoiling farmer scowled.

"Triumph!" growled the knight, in turmoil.

"Gold — !"
"Crops — !"
"Victory — !"

The knight glared at the banker, glared at the farmer, glared the banker, back to farmer back to banker back to knight.

For split seconds a fistfight threatened.

It was the knight set matters all right.

"It means much," he said, instead.

"Much," conceded the farmer, eased.

"Double much!" The banker sneezed.

"Much indeed!" the knight decreed, with which the three achieved agreement.

"Thus," proceeded the knight in delight. "I myself must muster you in!"

"Today the King convenes his council. I'll get the facts to him exactly!"

The knight snapped upright in the saddle. He clapped the catch of his vizor tight.

Then, spurring his steed to a stirring trot, he raced to the top of the scurrying party, and paced before it, high and mighty.

The farmer muttered.

The banker sputtered.

Meanwhile Wyeth, settling back, took the din and hubbub in, as calm as calm could be.

CHAPTER
I:II

Who saw the troupe go flying by was startled, stumped or mystified. For none could guess what could unite a farmer, woodman, banker, knight.

First the knight came into sight, candy-bright in bands of sunlight.
At his heels the banker wheeled, scheming steals and seamy deals.
Next the farmer's creaking cart, with Wyeth speaking from the heart.
Who heard his speech set off in a streak. Rich and poor men, dukes to door-men — folk of high and low degree — enlisted after eagerly.
Thus the cortege queued and grew.
So when the town drew into view some hundreds strong clung close along, disputing, loud and rowdy.
Ditto through the thoroughfares.

Likewise downtown towards the Royal Square.
Where, there the gloomy castle loomed, bulking through the roomy air.

The knight, aflame with untamed pride, reined his straining stallion in, before the castle gates.
The others halted by him.

The swelling crowd, which milled about, greeted the group with jubilant shouts, and cheers, and tears of welcome.

When then a bumptious trumpet shrilled.
A chilling pair of trombones trilled.
A blare of snare-drums filled the air.

The banker rose.

The farmer froze.

Uptight, the knight stood up on tip-toes.

As Wyeth flushed the crowd hushed down, in expectation of the Crown.

But then, with no more explanation, the castle gates came sailing back, and squads of hard-boiled guards barged out — then charged, with truncheons flailing!

The howling crowd was shattered, then scattered, whereas the woodman stood his ground.

To start, the guards circled the cart. The startled farmer they parked apart.

They grabbed the woodman. They dragged him down. They bound his sinewy arms around.

The farmer covered in perspiration.

The knight shuddered in consternation.

The banker bordered on utter prostration.

Then, hands fast, Wyeth was made to dash through the Square and the castle gates, whose bolts crashed shut behind him.

A violent silence settled in.

The banker breathed. His windpipe wheezed.

Freezing his knees at twenty degrees, he bent back, body slack, nerves snapped, then blacked out.

CHAPTER
I:III

A stingling stick of the shrewd sword-tips sent the woodman tripping through the gates.

The bolts shot shut. The woodman got up. At which the guards, gripping their charge, marched him through the cobbled courtyard.

They tracked through vast but vacant places lacking, oddly, living traces. Spacious halls. Gracious malls. Galleries tall with vaulted walls.

Withal the woodman had the notion unseen eyes watched every motion.

When then they neared an arch, within which steps descended, darkly.

The guards took them two at a time.

The winding steps got steep, then steeper. Gloom closed in. Slime got deeper.

Then the party, rounding a bend, baulked before a doored dead-end.

Wyeth went cold to lo and behold:

MAXIMUM

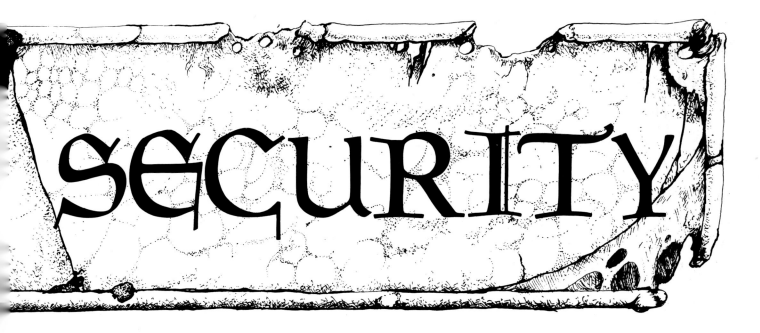

SECURITY

A guard gave three grave raps.

Whereat the squeaking door tore back, revealing an eye-patched gaoler, leering.

His teeth were black. His eye-piece patched. His torso, bare above the waist, was hairy flesh all over the place.

From his bloat throat hung baggy dewlaps. His shaggy arms dragged past vast kneecaps.

He was a chap of capital girth.

"Hark!" He barked. His dark teeth gnashed. "The arch-traitor at last!"

"Traitor —!"

Wyeth gasped. The gaoler laughed. Then grasped the woodman past the door.

And, after the guards had discharged out, he locked the door, on four scored sockets.

The gaoler jerked towards the woodman.

"You'll see what comes from trouble-making!"

"It's all a big mistake!" cried Wyeth, making a shakey gesture of protest.

The gaoler chuckled, gruffly.

"Bunk!" He scoffed, through blackened stumps. "That mangy tune you'll change, and soon!"

Crushed, the gloom-struck woodman hushed.

At which the gaoler, slashing the woodman's fetters off, slapped an oaken cell-door back, then clapped his captive within.

The gaoler's footfall faded off.

Stunned, the shell-shocked woodman stood, rocking to and fro.

The cell was small. Its stone walls wet. The floor was spread with shreds of straw. A wooden bench stood by the door.

Above, a tacked-up scroll extolled:

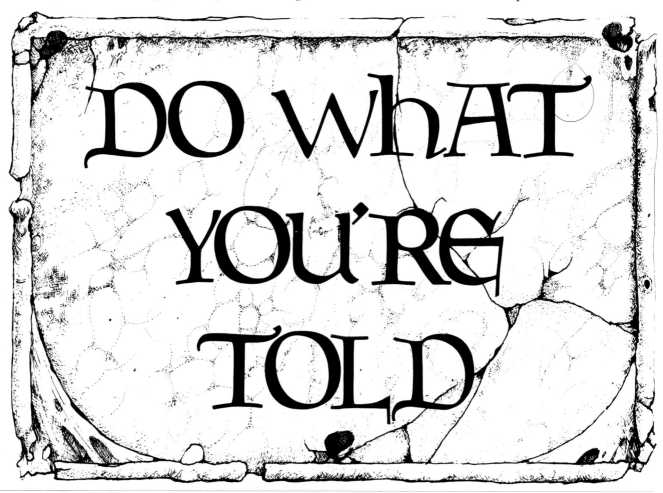

Wyeth's retinas rolled.

The woodman, wobbly, sprawled
down flat, to try to work out
what was what.

He fussed and tossed on his
musty bed. He scratched the back
of his aching head.

His brain pained. The world
waned. The farmer, banker, knight
complained.

And, as his feelings slowly
sank, the woodman's reeling mind
went blank.

Then Wyeth sensed his shoulder
shaken. His arm, flung out, felt
wrung or taken.

The woodman stirred. His eyes
unblurred.

Whereat, in a flash, he whirled
awake, coming aware of an eerie shape.
Above, it hovered, peering down,
face half-hid in the drapes of a cape!

A shock tocked through the
woodman.

The noble nose. . . . The winning
chin. . . . The thin beguiling profile
smiling. . . .

"It's *you* —!"

Wyeth leaped to his feet.

"Hush —!" the other softly said,
touching a fingertip to his lip. "For none
must know that I've come."

Instantly Wyeth arrested.

Wherewith the other, reaching within
the folds of his cloak, swiftly withdrew a
silver key. He held it high that Wyeth see,
then slipped it into the lock.

The door tipped back a crack.

Wyeth jumped. For, there before the
opened door, the fuddled gaoler lay
out-stretched, snoring soundly, snout
wine-wet.

A half-drained wine cask stood
untended, while empty ale flasks lay
up-ended.

The gaoler's gurgling belly babbled.

Wyeth smiled. Grave, the other gazed a
while. Then waved the woodman onward.

Breathing hollow, Wyeth followed.

They stole around the sounding
gaoler. Then tip-toed towards the outer
door, which clicked ajar as the one before.

Then up the stairs. Out the entry. Past
a pair of dozing sentries.

The fair night air repaired the
woodman.

And then, in a trice, the two took flight.

Skirting the castle's crown of lights,
skimming a shimmering skein of heights,
they spiraled high through the glimmering
night toward the rim of the star-shot sky,
and the gliding scythe of the quarter moon.

Ghostly, they coasted forward.

A bell would knell. An owl hoot.
A cockerel crow, or sleepless hoopoe.

Then, sailing above the moon-pale
fields, dotted with silvery rocks and
treetops, wails were heard of forlorn
birds, mournful grunts of prey or hunter,
and whistling quail in bristling brambles.

And then they alit in a drift of
thick mist.

With which the other, wheeling
about, peeled off the cape had hitherto
concealed him.

Wyeth gaped. Blood whipped to his
tingling face.

For, bright in a nimbus of singing
light, there stood the radiant shape of
a Prince —!

CHAPTER
II

CHAPTER
II:I

The Prince stood bright before the woodcutter, ringed in singing cycles of light.

His jacket was gold, with silver, in folds. His satin breeches were trimmed with pearl. His purple cape, furled at his feet, curled over the tips of his glistering slippers.

The Prince was instinct with invincible radiance.

"Who are you, then," the woodcutter whispered.

"My name is Yvian," the Prince declared, voice like a bell in the clear night air. "And I—and no other—am the rightful ruler of this land."

Wyeth's quavering heart gave a start.

"Long ago I was enchanted—confined to the cabined trunks of the trees from dawn until the dusk; but by night free to wander at large to seek the one who might perchance release me from my spell."

"What—?"

"Listen closely," implored the Prince, before embarking on his dark tale.

"Long ago I reigned, Wyeth, much longer than you might suppose, for an enchanted creature is perpetually young. My mother the Queen I never knew, as that good dame died in the childbirth of which I was the issue. My father I loved and revered. He was a just and sagacious King who ruled the land wisely and well. Beloved by his subjects, dear to his friends, respected by sovereigns far and wide, he was ever a tender parent to me. On that sad day of his death I, his only son and heir, was destined to ascend to his power and dignity, and but for my wicked uncle Ulphius surely would have done so.

"Yet long had Ulphius coveted the crown, and plotted to pluck it to his bosom. To this end he had struck a bargain with the three Black Sisters of the forest, Glattisynge, Gruccynge and Gyffyn. Against certain favours, to be granted after their schemes were carried out, the sisters agreed to spirit me away, to slay me secretly in the forest, disappearing without a trace, thereby leaving the throne and prerogatives vacant for Ulphius to fall heir to.

"So that late one night shortly after my father's death, while court and kingdom slept in sorrow, the heavens themselves feigning sable, the sisters stole from their dwellingplace deep in the forest, mounted their broomsticks and soared aloft, bound for the royal castle.

"It was a dismal night. A black wind

moaned and rattled the trees, skipping dead leaves along deserted country lanes. Lonely dogs bayed at the moon. Nightbirds kept close to their nests. Good men tossed and shuddered in their sleep, hugging the quilts tighter about their shoulders. None dared move or stir abroad, save goblins, elves or other imps bent on tricks or mischief.

"At the final stroke of midnight the sisters emerged from a cloudbank. Gliding down, they circled the castle, then slipped through the narrow casement of my bed chamber, high atop the Western tower. I heard a faint rustling sound and perceived three gloomy figures draped in black hunched in a far corner of the room. Sure they were my good nurses come to look to my safety and welfare, I drew myself up, called softly out, and beckoned them to my side.

"The witches crept forward, and I reached out my arms to embrace them. But *alas!* instead of the kind voices of my guardians I heard a horrid triple-chortle that froze the blood in my veins. In a flash the hags had seized upon me. They crammed me into a black velvet bag, fastened the cords, hung the sack on the butt of a broomstick. Then, on the heels of a flying leap, they whisked me out into the vacant night, where struggles and cries, had I been capable of them, would have availed me nothing.

"I lay in that bag for what seemed an

age, huddled and helpless, faint with terror and nameless dread, compelled withal to hear the witches cackling and their shrieks of glee as they hurtled across the trackless sky, bearing their luckless load.

"At length we alighted in the forest. (This I knew from the chatter of insects and the hoots of owls.) The witches, snickering, hobbled on, dragging the sack and its contents behind, causing me to suffer many cruel bruises. We reached a glade, and here the crones opened the bag and pitched me out onto the ground.

"Trembling, I lay at their feet, unable to speak, half dead with fright. The eldest witch, Glattisynge—a hag horrible to behold with her chalky skin speckled with warts and crooked nose that hooked beneath her leprous lips to the tip of her stubbly chin—she, Glattisynge, withdrew a willow wand from the false top of her broomstick and, hissing a charm, circum-scribed a magic circle close about my heart.

"At once the crickets quit their lyrical song; rooks and night-jars, tremulous, fell silent; and raccoons and foxes padded through the brush to hide in their bushy tails.

"A moan then shuddered through the forest. Black clouds drifted across the moon: a moment later they broke to bare a lunar orb stained a rich incarnadine. Its rays dropped gules upon the toothless gums of the witches; lumined like buttons the eyes of toads crouched in the ferns around us; badged with scarlet the claws of bats now wheeling and cheeping in our midst.

"The sisters screeched in delight. Gruccynge snatched a glowing coal from a pocket concealed in her cape. She touched it to a heap of faggots set in a hollow nearby. At once there shot up a jade-green flame, while coal-black sparks went whizzing and scribbling, and popped in every direction. Yet, though I lay close, near touching the blaze I stiffened, then shook, then grew numb with cold, for the sparks struck chill as snow or hail, the tongues of flame as bitter as ice.

"Clucking contentedly, Gruccynge replaced the coal in her pocket. She slid her thumbs twixt her bloodless chaps and, fetching breath, whistled sharply. Straightway Gyffyn—the youngest sister but no less hideous—produced a curious crystal vial that seethed and bubbled with quicksilver. Sneering, she circled the glade, laying the ground with a glistering hoop of bubbling, mercurial quicksilver. Then, flinging her withered arms straight out, she snapped her fingers, twiddling her toes, whereon the silver too flashed to flame, this of yellow, and purging a murky bluish smoke.

"With a yelp of joy, the sisters bounded beside me. They intertwined their corky fingers, cocked their heads,

cackling raucously, and proceeded to dance in wild abandon. Their night-dark capes fluttered in the wind; their crinkly hair bristled beneath their cone-shaped bonnets; their leather sandals scarce touched the ground; their flying figures merged to black blurs. Nor did the hags fatigue or falter until the waning moon had set—a red saucer in a dubious sky— at which they turned to me once more, now with deadly intent.

"I thought my end was sure at hand, and already was offering up my prayers when a strange thing came to pass.

"Suddenly Gyffyn let go an ear-piercing shriek. A whistle then, and a cluck of her raspy tongue.

"'Sisters!' cried she. 'Why should we take the Prince's life when we ourselves might use him? Whether he lives is nothing to Ulphius so long as the Prince is got rid of! And if the King is none the wiser, still from him we'll get our guerdon and have us a Prince to boot!

"'At our command he'll spark our fire in the chill of dawn; stir the porridge; grind the mustard. He'll skin our cheese and press the eggshells! Preen our cats and comb their tails! He'll pepper the yard and spice our ale!

"'Why, we'll need but rub our thumbs and all our wants shall straight be done! By whom? The Prince, the late King's son!'

"At that a volatile current thrilled

through the witches. Their eyes burned with an eager flame. Their pointy ears tingled and sparked. Their lips twitched, and spittle slid down. And then their shrivelled trunks went limp, luxurious with longing.

"Suddenly the velvet sack again environed me; again we spiraled into giddy flight; again we streaked through the boundless sky: and when next released I found myself in the sisters' domain, uncharted leagues in the heart of the forest.

"In their hut the sisters lost no time in habiting me in the coarse weeds of a servant. They rent my princely raiment, dabbed it with mire, then raddled it through with the blood of a fresh-slain hind. These tatters they presented to the new King as proof the lethal act was done. Indeed, so pleased was Ulphius that he rewarded the sisters with a bonus chest of precious stones and, according to agreement, pledged his protection in all their dark transactions. Well satisfied, the sisters took their leave and returned to their hut in the forest.

"There I lived for many years, rich in the knowledge of my regal heritage, yet a menial to the three beldames. Against their potent craft I was helpless, and so I resolved to accept my new life — though it was that of a churl and caitiff — grateful, indeed, to have life at all.

"Yet my lot was a hard one. I slept in

a ruined henhouse in the yard, a leaky roof to ward the rain, a hingeless door to fend the ruffling blasts of winter. The sagging windows were rotten and cracked, the worm-riddled walls about to buckle. In spring the damp clay floor was ooze, while winter sheened it with a patina of ice. In a litter of musty straw I bedded, my only cover a decayed goat-skin, one so worn, so patched and holey there was more patch than skin, and a bare bit of that, for its bald surface scanted the edges even of my diminished body.

"I rose before the break of dawn to perform daylong the witches' service. The chores were harsh, the labour endless, and rest or respite disallowed me. Only long past dusk could I creep back to my wretched coop, my sole reward a shallow bowl of watery soup and a stale crust of bread to sup on. No day of repose or leisure was mine, for the witches scorned our Sunday sabbath, nor did they venerate any season save All Hallow's Eve and Friday the Thirteenth.

"Yet never was I able to do enough, and nothing I did was thought well done. I drudged till body and soul were sore, and still the sisters found fault in all. My pains won nought but check and rebuff. My toil was meted with cold contempt. Redoubled, my efforts were paid by thumps. And often when skittish or merely for sport the witches would slap

my tender shins or smartly pinch my ears.

"Nevertheless I determined to keep my spirits from flagging. I did as told, and did so with cheer. When punished or put on still shorter rations, I allowed no plaint to escape my lips. When scolded or struck, however cruelly, I held my tongue and persevered. My hours of sleep, already few, I curtailed still further, on my own, solely to advance the witches' comfort. But above all else I clung to my faith that no creature, however benighted, could forever prevail in wickedness.

"For no small while my hopes proved vain. Indeed, I had almost given over thought of change when, imperceptibly, the rude manners of the witches softened.

"One night I was suffered to enter their hut and lay my blanket beside their fire. The ensuing month I was let again, and again the fortnight following. When the wind whistled through the chinks of my hovel a woollen coverlet was mine to snuggle in. By day I was given an extra breadcrust; and later on the crumb. Sometimes at dusk I was doled out nuts; on one rare feast day fruit. The cuffs and snarls of the witches waned and eventually were no more.

"And then the strangest of things occurred, one which I, even most sanguine, had never dared to hope.

"For these wierd women, who hated with a burning hatred all things of heaven and earth — excepting themselves and

their cats—why, the witches seemed to hate me no longer. Indeed, the faint impression crept upon me that the sisters actually had come to *like* me—and little more could possibly have been said for the poor things since love, by its inner nature and theirs, was forever denied them.

"But about that time the sisters began to feel the effects of their awful age. For, although a witch may live a full thousand years, that span by, she must needs weaken and die. So it fell out that the eldest sister, Glattisynge, dizzied one day and, while quaffing a spirited elixir, dropped the goblet and suddenly expired.

"Now, being a witch, Glattisynge had neither blood nor soul, and at her demise instantly dissolved into a palmful of dust and ashes. Weeping tearlessly (witches may not cry), the two surviving sisters gathered the residue, taking infinite care to overlook no speck. Depositing all in a leathern pouch, they soared aloft, arm in arm, and, wailing, scattered to the vagabond winds the pittance of powder that so recently had made the stuff of their sister, Glattisynge.

"The witch's death cast great gloom on her kin and, truth to tell, upon myself. For weeks we found but little to say, and though we did our daily rounds we all were heavy at heart. Yet even then, while cuddling her cats, Blast and Mephisto, a startled cry escaped Gruccynge. Striken, she too fell and, in a twinkling of an eye, crumbled to ashes and dust. With a breathless moan, Gyffyn scooped up the tiny heap and, flying far beyond the clouds, dealt the meagre palmful of matter to the eternal company of the restless winds.

"On coasting down Gyffyn called me to her side. Her voice seemed plangent, grave, sepulchral. Leaning nervously on the butt of her broomstick, she spoke at last of the years gone by. She called to mind our first encounter in the glade, recollected my long detention in the witches' company. Avoiding my eyes, she said that my example had deeply shamed the sisters. Only after I had come amongst them, said Gyffyn, had the sisters glimpsed true happiness. Stung by remorse, the three had lain awake many a night striving to find a way to make amends for their sins.

"Above all they had wished to restore me to my rightful place in the kingdom. But, said Gyffyn, a black deed done is not so easily undone. There was but a single and precarious path to my restoration — I was to submit to an enchantment; and both the spell and its means of breaking had to be chosen by my mortal enemy, Ulphius.

"An icy shiver scuttled up my spine as I heard this dreaded name. Trembling, I asked that Gyffyn divulge the charm. But, lips sealed, she turned away to enter

her hut, whose precincts were forfended me the first time in a goodly while.

"For three days and nights entire the witch remained within, busily plying her art. The door was barred, the windows fastened. Black smoke puffed and curled from the chimney, and her mumbled chants and incantations echoed far and wide over the countryside. Again I slept in my draughty hovel, nourishing myself on hips and haws whilst awaiting Gyffyn's summons.

"Finally, on the morning of the fourth day the fumes of a quickness ceased. The hut and countryside fell strangely silent. Filled with foreboding, I awaited word from Gyffyn until, nibbled by impatience, I could wait no longer. I tried the door. To my surprise it slowly creaked ajar. I crossed the threshold, only to utter a cry of distress. For, there, stretched weakly across the hearthstones, Gyffyn lay, breathing hoarsely.

"I rushed forward, bent over to aid her. But, forcing her leaden eyelids open, the ancient witch but shook her head and implored me to hear her diligently.

"Her conjurations, she whispered, were now complete, and that very midnight the new spell would take effect. Then she revealed the charm and its secret, and for all she begged forgiveness. Adding that she was suffering from the sudden brittleness that heralded her death, she asked that I dispose of her remains as she had those of her sisters.

"To all this I gave my ready assent, and with it poured much sorrow and tears. For then it was I understood that, although poor Gyffyn could no more than like me, I had actually grown to love her. But on the instant she perished. And upon the hearthstones where a moment before Gyffyn had lain, I could discover nothing more than a palmful of dust and ashes.

"This I painstakingly collected and deposited in the pouch. I returned to the glade where we had had our initial encounter. Then, climbing to the topmost branch of the very tree that towers above us now, Wyeth, I loosed the binders of the leathern pouch and let its powders go floating free for all the posting winds of heaven to catch and carry to the end of the creaking earth. I scarce had a breath to descend before midnight struck and my charm caught hold.

"And true to the words of sister Gyffyn, the King's enchantment has remained inviolate until this very day.

"What's to be done? Who can help? How can the spell be overcome?"

The woodman's pounding heart was sounding.

"Why are you called **The Honest Woodcutter?**" the Prince enquired, with underlying fire.

"Because I love the truth!" cried Wyeth. "But what does that matter now?"

The Prince side-stepped the woodman's question.

"And is there nothing you love as much?"

"Why, no!" replied the woodman, glowing. "I love the truth above all else! Still—! What does that matter now?"

"More than *anything*...?" the Prince persisted.

"Why, more than life itself!" cried Wyeth, clenching a calloused fist, intensely.

The Prince expelled a telling breath.

"Then you alone," he stated, then waited. "Possess the power to break the spell."

"Me—?"

"Hearken closely," the Prince implored, before embarking on a starker tale.

CHAPTER
II:II

"Good Wyeth, retrieve with me the day that Ulphius learned I was not slain, but lived, a bondsman to the witches and, now free, was destined to be charmed.

"These tidings lashed the King to fury. He stamped his feet. He gnashed his teeth. He pounded a fist in his sweaty palm and clamoured for revenge. And yet his fit, still hot, subsided, mastered by his iron cunning. Swearing to rivet his crown forever beyond the stroke or blast of fortune, the King retired to his secret sanctum, sunk beneath the inmost castle, there to pursue his dark researches.

"In that close and fetid cuddy arrasses hung the granite walls; carpets muffled the marble floor; a solitary taper burned; and deadly silence stopped the ears. A crystal ball and hour-glass were posed upon an ebony table; and closets and cabinets, which packed the walls, were laden with yellowing volumes and parchments—clandestine texts of the forbidden art.

"Bolting the door, of which he alone

possessed the key, the King took up a massy folio and set himself to study.

"First he certained there was no option but yield to my enchantment (this by the law of the black art); then assured that one way only could ever break the spell (this by the quality of enchantments); and lastly he confirmed his right (as party to a muted pact) to name the charm, its pain and privilege, and prescribe its taking-off.

"Decocting all, the King lapsed into meditation. From this deep state he did not stir throughout the long and tedious night, nor past the sequent noon. A wraith-like smile then creased his lips. He sneered, then snickered in satisfaction. At length he rose, summoned retainers, and issued certain instructions. Only then did the moody sovereign fill full a stoup of purple wine and, sipping, stare at the hour-glass until the utmost grain dropped midnight.

"Suddenly a crippling wind shivered the chamber, flickering the taper, spinning the hour-glass, and fluttering the sheets of the tome before him. The crystal ball glowed icy white, then flashed, then turned stark black. Wherewith, from out of the crystal's fathomless depths there loomed the face of sister Gyffyn.

"A knock ensued, a stupendous clatter. And as the thrice-locked door blew back, the King beheld the witch herself, lapped in night-dark velvet.

"Hobbling forward, she demanded to

know the terms of my charm. Without a word Ulphius delivered a wax-sealed scroll which Gyffyn tore open at once. At first she smiled. Then she frowned. And then the witch went black as coal, while apprehension grappled her heart.

"For, the King, once hitting on my tree-bound charm, had fixed as ransom not the customed doughty deed, as raising a mount from the bottomless sea, or plaiting the locks of the serpent-crowned Medusa. Instead he contrived a canny test, particular in singularity: — that I make questionless proof that indeed there lived someone who loved the truth more than life itself.

"In sudden disgust Gyffyn spat out a stream of sparks that scorched the scroll, singed the rugs, and set the King's red beard to smouldering. And yet the monarch, savouring the moment, snapped his fingers beneath her nose and laughed the witch to scorn. Packing his oily palms together, he swore the charm could not be broken — no, not till blizzards engulfed the sands of the desert, and orchids spiced the snow-driven poles.

"A mournful sob broke from Gyffyn's breast as sadly she shuffled towards the door. In a blast of boiling wind she vanished. But behind, the sulphurous air eddied and seethed, toppling the glass, dropping a heavy arras in a heap, dousing the taper, and dealing the King to darkness. Yet, howling his bliss to the

steamy air, the jubilant King repaired to the court, convinced the crown was his forever.

"That very day he decreed a feast; and revels and masques, mimes and mirths were performed in Ulphius' sovereign honour.

"Three nights later my enchantment took hold, and I set out, confident that real love, so far from being more precious than pearl, was as plentiful as acorns in a forest of oak.

"At the first opportunity I sought out the home of the burgher, Fluett, a gentleman renowned for charity, humility and love of his fellows.

"As doer of good and humane deeds, the burgher's name was amongst the foremost. As giver of alms and help to the down-trodden, Fluett was ever the first to be called on. As prop and pillar to those in need, Master Fluett stood second to none. Those in extremity flocked to his door, never departing empty-handed. Yet, in keeping with his selfless nature, Master Fluett eschewed the limelight. Living modestly, working quietly, Fluett, withal, was of legendary repute. His good name I had heard even on the lips of the witches, and thus felt certain that this benefactor would welcome the chance of breaking my spell.

"Fluett lived in a splendid estate not far from the castle itself. At once I was struck by the beauty of the holdings, and my heart leapt up at this evidence of merit so amply rewarded. The approaches were ornate, the door imposing, the gleaming brass knocker so huge and weighty I scarce was able to budge it. Still, I managed, and to my delight the burgher himself stood before me.

"Fluett received me readily. Rather obese, richly though soberly attired, with watery eyes and a windy voice, he ushered me into an ante-room, where he listened attentively to my tale. As I recited he muttered or mumbled; from time to time he wisely winked; once or twice he nodded assent; all the while he puffed and pulled on his amber pipe, and the room soon swirled with aromatic smoke.

"On reaching the end of my tale, I leaned forward, breathless to hear his response.

"But, strange to say, only an awkward pause ensued. The burgher blinked. He stared up dully. He wiped his watery eyes. He blew his bulbous nose. Stranger still, he yawned. Then, strangest of all, pocketing his lacey handkerchief, he wheezed the single syllable *Ahhh*.... With which he rose, dug his needley fingers into my arm, and directed me towards the door.

"I turned questioningly. But without ado or apology, the burgher abruptly thrust me out. I knocked again, thinking there had been some mistake.

"After a moment a heavy bolt slid into place. A key turned. The lock clicked.

The coach lights dimmed, then winked straight off. Next, a voice I recognized as Fluett's gruffly ordered me gone.

"Puzzled at this remarkable behaviour, I lingered some while before his steps, then repaired, baffled, to the forest.

"Yet I was not disheartened. True, I had failed—doubtless due to my own omissions—to convey my meaning to Master Fluett. But all would be different with the worthy Flymm, a titled citizen whose honour, kindness and generosity were fabled throughout the land.

As tireless promotor of the general good, the name of Flymm was held in awe. As mover of glorious public works, Flymm was acclaimed in the highest circles. As benevolent patron and unstinting donor, Flymm was trumpeted for spontaneous munificence.

"Chapels, hospitals, libraries, colleges, and other grand projects too numerous to mention were standing monuments to his wisdom and bounty. Yet, though Flymm was preoccupied with mighty endeavours, no human problem was too minute for his judicious assessment. Thus I set out the very next night, convinced that a spirit of such largess would seize the occasion to end my charm.

"Flymm was a short fleshy man who occupied a manor grander even than that of Fluett. Admittance he granted without reserve. And yet, as we proceeded through his lavish dwelling, I gained an

impression, willy-nilly, which ill-accorded with his repute.

"Perhaps his stiff and studied gait seemed more a march or stilted strut. Perhaps it was his shifty eyes which peered but never met my gaze. It might have been his style of dress, outwardly plain, which on more careful scanning revealed as plush or even foppish. But I quickly dismissed such thoughts, attributing them to my want of experience.

"At last we reached Flymm's wainscotted study, where I commenced my recitation. But part way through I became aware that the great man payed scant attention. Rather his eyes were darting back and forth, playing over the objects of price — the ivories, jades, rare silks and crystals — that filled his mansion to overflowing. Surely, I thought, he was restive to hear the end of my story, that he might help the sooner. Thus I summed up and concluded rapidly, though omitting no vital matter.

"After a moment Flymm got up. Creaking, he bowed. He thanked me for an hour of diversion. Tapping a knuckle on a vast polished table, he asked — extremely reluctantly — if I required a copper for my pains.

"Unable to credit my ears, I rose. At which Flymm, grasping my shoulder in a grip like steel rods, marched me from the study.

"Through room on room I passed

deferringly, my eyes downcast, daring no peep. Before the door I meekly hesitated. At that the burgher's body snapped rigid. His neck and puffy face turned purple. He threw back the door, advancing precipitiously. Then, bashing me squarely across the bottom, he sent me flying from the house.

"The door slammed. Startled, I stood rubbing my hurt — at which an oath, vile, unrepeatable, came hissing through the keyhole. Horrified, I froze. Whereat a fresh invective, fouler by far than the first, bludgeoned my unbelieving ears.

"The door flew open. Brandishing a club, a livid Flymm came sprinting toward me, his face distorted with rage. I spun about, just managing to dodge a flail of his club, and instantly took to my heels. Flymm charged after me. But soon I outdistanced my slow-footed pursuer, leaving him puffing and cursing behind. After which — bewildered by his extraordinary deportment — I slowly retreated to the forest.

"I passed the whole of the following day examining my conduct, trying to detect my fault. Surely, I thought, my long years amongst the witches had roughened or deadened my sensibilities. The two good burghers had taken offence at some crude gaffe I had unwittingly perpetrated. I had been tactless or remiss in some essential show of courtesy. Some quillet or subtle incivility had, unbeknownst to me, given umbrage. Perhaps — so long had I been removed from correct society — I had been downright oafish.

"Reflection convinced me it could not have been otherwise. To Fluett and Flymm I would make amends. But now, fired afresh, I longed to be loose so as to be able to solicit the nobleman Flaskett, a grandee renowned throughout the earth for wisdom, justice, toleration, and his profound understanding of human nature.

"Divines and scholars from every quarter flocked to Flaskett for advice and counsel. Delegations from distant continents would cross the oceans to crave his assistance. Sages and saints from the antipodes would traverse vast jungles and mountain ranges, struggle through bleak and barren ice caps, undergoing unspeakable hardship, only to lay their arcane mysteries at the nobleman's feet. None was deceived or left unenlightened. Flaskett, I knew, would hear me out with quiet compassion, comprehend as no other could, and, sure to digest my knotty problems, still was to be counted upon to make allowance for my shortcomings.

"Nevertheless, before setting out, I took the precaution of reviewing once more all proper forms and usage; after which I felt radiantly certain that such a spirit would be overjoyed at the opportunity of terminating my enchantment.

"Flaskett's house was nothing smaller

than the royal castle, and compassed round by gardens and fountains rivaling those of the King. A gold-crested gate accessed to his park, which stretched as far as the eye could see. Stables and out-buildings, graced with lawns and fantastical hedgerows, were set in fresh and fragrant arbours. Pavilions and pleasure-domes crowded the skyline, crowning magnificent alleys of elms. A broad and stately carriageway, which wound through a fret-work of silver canals, mounted gently towards his door, where a liveried footman answered my knock.

"Just then Flaskett himself appeared. He was excessively tall and lean, wore a waxed goatee, and possessed a pair of lynx-like eyes that narrowed to two sharp points. Straight as a ramrod, as stiff he stood, garbed in a glittering riding habit which, I could not but note, was of a late and military cut. I bowed, wishing to over-look no etiquette. Yet, before I could speak a word, Flaskett, who measured twice my size, laid hands upon my collar.

"Mildly, I tried to draw back. But Flaskett shook me all the more roughly. He ripped my jacket, tore off the buttons, slashed and shredded my cape and breeches. he shoved and bullied me, crushing my toes. He rained blows and abuse upon me.

"Dazed, I staggered, sinking to my knees. Venting a brutal shriek of pleasure, Flaskett kicked me viciously. I fell flat.

Flaskett lashed me with his riding crop. He ran the rowels of his silver spurs across the raw of my lacerated calf. He lashed again, and yet again until a pattern of scarlet welts stood proud upon my tender skin.

"I nearly swooned. Whereat the nobleman, commanding his servants to clear the way—which task they expeditiously accomplished—scooped me up by the seat of my trousers and, like some weight of loathsome baggage, hurled me out into the moonless night.

"I lay at his doorstep, heaving with sobs —less from pain than humiliation—at which I suffered the further indignity of Flaskett tarring his hounds upon me.

"Snarling and nipping, a savage pack of mastiffs stormed over me, clawing and bruising from every quarter. At once I fled, eluding with difficulty my rabid assailants, and not without leaving my cape and a patch of my tattered britches to the slavering jaws of the hounds. For the following day and for weeks thereafter I remained in the sanctuary of the forest, brooding on my disgrace.

"I had done nothing to merit such treatment. I had said no word. I had even bowed as Flaskett entered the hall. Yet he had spurned me most harshly out. Never, not in my darkest dreams, had I imagined such an action possible. The witches themselves at their worst had never used me with such promiscuous malice. Then it was that I began to suspect that neither Flaskett, nor Fluett, nor Flymm was the gentleman commonly supposed.

"Thus I resolved to search out more ordinary folk, and for months on end consorted with cobblers, bakers, bricklayers — every class and cut of person — hoping to find but one amongst them willing to break my enchantment. Though these kind people shared with me what bread they had, harbouring me so long as I liked, still, not one was to be found who would consider assisting me.

"Despondent, I quit the towns and took to wandering the countryside. I spoke with shepherds, vintners, gentry. I parleyed with pilgrims, hermits, nomads, but always to no avail. Further I strayed, and further still, visiting strange and curious lands, witnessing mighty and calamitous events. But to whomsoever I spoke, woefully, the response was ever the same.

"At length, weary, hopeless — disillusioned not disenchanted — I betook myself to my forest refuge, not knowing whither else to turn. And there it was, deep in my own country and heartland, that first I chanced to hear your name and learn your good report, Wyeth.

"Instantly my heart pounded. I lept up, combed the surroundings, hastened to seek you out: — and from the first moment I beheld your face knew the instrument of my deliverance."

"He can't get away with it!" Wyeth wailed, pale at the Prince's harrowing tale. "We'll show the King, make him know he's wrong!"

Long the Prince surveyed him, gravely.

"*You*," said he, peculiar in tone. "For *you* it must be, and *you* alone. . . ."

The woodman blinked at the wrinkling Prince.

With which the latter swept a hand, East, towards the line of the defining horizon.

"Behold," he said, uneasily. "Even now the dawn creeps near; and from the coming of that hour it is forbidden we meet again until the King's fell spell is broken. . . ."

The Prince paced back. Some lustre lacked.

"That too," he sighed, with downcast eyes, "the King in his cunning has specified. . . ."

Yvian suddenly seemed colder, and older. He faltered, then fell silent.

"Then I'll go it alone!" the woodman cried, plying his dauntless eyes towards the sky.

"And when the King has got his due, why, we two shall meet on the other side!"

The woodman struck a plucky posture.

The Prince reached out. The woodman's hand he took in his.

"So be it," said he, perfervidly.

Then, lifting an arm in valediction, Yvian drew back, and suddenly vanished.

Again the wondering woodman blinked. When then, in a trice, again he took flight.

From mist which whistled with calls of quail, and wails he heard of stirring birds, he rose through the glimmering veins of the night, skimming the shimmering trees at height, over a whitening countryside, hushed with the breathless blush of morning.

Ghostly, he coasted forward.

A blue-jay flew. A cockerel crew. A newly-wakened cockatoo cuckooed.

Then, rising high towards the coppery sky, daubed with russet tufts of cloud-puffs, Wyeth was swirled and wafted and whirled towards the curve of the swerving world, the dimming fires of the morning star, and the far-off spires of the oncoming town.

And then the woodman seemed to swoon; and, swooning, seemed to plummet down; down through hoops of golden crowns, rained with elemental sound, and loops and haloes of singing light.

And Wyeth shook his tingling head; and felt a twinge akin to dread: for, looking round, he found himself once again within the walls of the King's appalling dungeon.

CHAPTER
III

CHAPTER
III:I

"Rise and shine!" The gaoler croaked, giving the woodman a poke for a joke.

"Day already . . . ?"

The gaoler shrugged. He shoved his mug towards where the sky was. Above, the woodman spied a pinch of sunlight struggling through a chink.

He blinked then backed to earth.

"But where's the Prince?" he cried, surprised, rising to his two's.

"What Prince—?"

"Yvian, dunce!" cried Wyeth at once. "We spent the night in the forest together!"

The gaoler jumped. His lips slipped back, in sticky chunks.

"Bunk!" He scoffed, through funky stumps. "Here you've been locked up all night! Right behind these bars!"

The bars he jarred convincingly.

"No!" cried Wyeth, in defiance. "The Prince and I, we flew far off! Why, I've only just got back!"

Stumped, the gaoler scratched, then stomped. Whereat his simian fingers snapped.

"Sure!" he cried, black eyes gone snide. "Plus Kings and Queens makes nice sweet dreams!"

The gaoler laughed, and loudly.

Wyeth scowled, too fouled to answer.

When then a great knock rocked the cell-block.

"The guard—!"

The gaoler listened long and hard. Then gave a shout. Then bounced about.

And, slipping a key off a clip at the hip, out he charged, while whistling crisply.

The door slammed shut behind him.

Wyeth's ear glued to the door.

Through, there blew a hue of voices. Too, a beat of booted feet. Shrieks as well, and weepy peeps. Also awesome squeaks, and beeps.

And then the uproar was no more. The boisterous buzz of voices ceased. Shrieks, then weepy beeps decreased. Also awful squeaks, and peeps.

Jackboots tapped a fleet retreat.

Seconds stretched, a score or less, before the door blew to.

Electrified, Wyeth clapped eyes on his friend the banker—brutalized!

"Wyeth!" He wept, beating his breast. "Me—! I am arrested!"

"Arrested?" echoed the woodman, weakly.

"Arrested!" bleated the banker, bleakly.

"Popped—!" The gaoler licked his chops, and bopped the banker within.

The banker staggered by the door. He skid a step or two, no more.

Then he sagged. An ankle snagged. An extra step he somehow dragged.

Whereat his flabby body flapped. And at the kneecaps he collapsed.

He lay there, wailing fraily.

Dismayed, the woodman made to aid him.

The gaoler scratched. His thatch he snatched. He picked a nit from a pitch-black patch.

Then, flicking the nit from a gritty thumb-tip, he split, while whistling a wicked limerick.

The door jammed shut behind him.

The banker lay in disarray, limp, a pimply bloated blimp.

Each chubby cheek was rubbed in mud. His tubby nose was clubbed, and greased. His dapper dress, once of the best, besmudged, appeared a perfect mess.

The banker frankly stank.

"Popped!" He panted, scant of breath, and grabbed and stabbed his baggy breasts.

"But what's the wrong you've done?"

"None!" the bilious banker big-gunned.

"The charge is that I'm one of your number! For that I'm seized, if you please! My grand standing notwithstanding! Despite my priceless pedigrees! My costly, countless excellencies!"

He let a pathetic peep escape.

"Dashed like a cashless piece of trash into this ghastly dungeon!"

The banker sank in rank self-pity.

"What of the others?" Wyeth enquired.

At that the cranky banker back-fired.

"I don't know or care one bit! For the King counts me—like you—a culprit! A thug, a mug, a common convict—! A con-man, crook, a counterfeit—!"

He twisted like a contortionist.

"Oh," he moaned. "Make no mistake! I tweaked my nose! Tore my clothes!— Groaned!—Grovelled!—Fell flat!"

Up the banker abruptly sat.

"Still he held in the last account all falls square on you, Wyeth—!"

"Me—?"

"The King decreed I'll not be freed unless—yes!—you agree to confess!"

"Confess . . . ?"

"The face—!"

"What of it . . . ?"

"Was faked—!"

"Faked—?"

"A phoney—!"

"A phoney—?"

"But sure it's all baloney!"

The banker risked a shifty wink.

"It was the way I said!" cried Wyeth, staring straight ahead.

The banker screwed his gruesome face up. He blew the bog of his soggy nose.

With a wily stare he dared declare: "Now is now! Then was then!" The banker hawed, then hemmed.

"I'm sorry" said Wyeth, so soberly. "For all the ills and ails I've caused."

Pale, the baleful woodman paused.

"Yet plainly know, come what come may, I can not—will not—lie."

The banker nearly died.

"Ow!" He howled, and fouled a jowl. "My fate waits in the balance! The truth—!"

He coughed, and lost a loose tooth.

"The truth counts less than naught!" Wyeth purged an urge to answer.

The banker wheezed. He bobbed to his knees. He seized the woodman's big toe, then squeezed.

He rubbed the stubs of his grubby chins down and up the woodman's shins.

"Wyeth!" he pled, and beggared his legs. "Just pledge the face was never, was not! When freed you'll be a grandee—

a hot shot!"

He flashed a stash of cold cash.

Wyeth retrieved from the banker's squeeze.

"I don't care a hoot for your loot! It's the truth I treasure—and the Prince!"

"The Prince . . . ?"

The banker blankly blinked.

"Right!" cried Wyeth incisively. "For the face I found engraved on the tree was none but that of Prince Yvian!"

The banker blankly blinked.

"H-how do you know?" he asked, in gasps.

"The Prince himself informed me!"

"—?"

"Exactly!"

The woodman glowed. He stood to tip-toes. With one terse burst he rehearsed the goings-on of the eve.

"The proof—?" contested the sceptical banker. "Can you produce a proof?"

"A proof . . . ?"

"Of course!" cantankerous, the banker rebuked. "Else it will never stand up!"

"Stand up . . . ? Where . . . ?"

"*Any* where!" the other outburst. "You must have signed a contract!"

"No . . ."

"He gave a token, then—? A key—?"

"No. . . ."

"A ring—? Some guarantee—?"

"No."

"A signet, or a seal—?"

"N-no."

"A coin to clinch the deal—?"

" . . . ?"

"—!"

"He gave his word!" Wyeth cried, beside, despite, himself, with pride.

"Pshaw—!"

The banker blew out a blast of breath. He re-ballooned his majestic chest.

Unheaped, he leaped to his feet.

"I see," he professed, then effervesced. "That it is naught that you know of the the world!"

The woodman eyed him, widely.

"Far less," was stressed, with celestial zest. "Inestimably less of its wondrous workings!"

The banker's rhetorical breast expanded. His oratorical hands demanded.

"For, minus testamentary testimony, how assess credibility? How compute the certitude of his verisimilitude?

"How calculate or adjudicate or validate or evaluate the state of his verbal veracity rate?"

In a transcendental pose he froze.

"Had you heard," said Wyeth quietly. "You would know the worth of his word."

The banker briskly dismissed it.

"It's nothing but a dream!"

"It was not!" cried Wyeth hotly. "The gaoler tried that too!"

"The gaoler . . . ?"

A beastly roar creased the door.

"You'd better believe it—!"

As one, the inmates spun about.

"Me, I kept the watch past break of day! Checked the woodman snoring away! Har! The gaoler didn't snooze a wink!"

A snort, short, ensued, of sorts.

"Now how do you think this chintzy Prince got in and out and out and in?"

Behind, designed a mindless grin.

"Rubbish!" Wyeth promptly put in. "You're the one who slept!"

The banker lept. His gooseflesh crept. His scalp ejected jets of sweat.

He turned sternly towards the gaoler.

"Bunk!" He scoffed, through funky stumps. "My orders are to watch awake! You think the gaoler would have slept?"

A raw guffaw gored the door.

The banker bawled. His looseflesh crawled. He sprawled against a wall, appalled.

He turned towards the woodman, sternly.

"Would the gaoler have slept—?"

"He did!" cried Wyeth indignantly. "First he drained a cask of wine! Next came flasks of ale!"

"Wine and ale—!"

The banker quailed. He gnawed his nails. His carked heart quasi failed.

He turned infirmly towards the goaler.

"Bunk!" He burped. The jail door lurched. "That's against the rules!"

Fists swished, for emphasis.

"Against the rules—!"

The banker wept. His cod-piece wet. His red neck flecked with abject sweat.

Unfirm, he turned towards the woodman.

"Dare the guardian of this station break, negate, or manipulate a stipulation of the regulations?"

He slumped, then bumped his sumptuous rump.

"He did!" cried Wyeth wildly. "He did! I know he did!"

The gaoler just giggled.

CHAPTER
III:II

When then a knock shocked through the dungeon.

"The guard—!"

The jumpy banker bumbled and babbled as the gaoler scrabbled off.

And sure enough gruff shouts broke out. Too, a rough tattoo of jackboots. Also puffs, and pules like mules. Now and then a swish or swoosh.

With which, as quick, the din desisted. Shouts, then bruit of boots died out. Pules, then swishes dis-persisted. Puffs and swooshes non-existed.

Sixty seconds trickled past before the door bashed to.

The banker shook. The looking woodman double-took.

For, at the door there groped some bloke wrapped top to toe in loops of rope!

Rope wound round a would-be head. Rope bound round two should-be legs. Roped the chest. Roped the tummy. The bloke was roped just like some mummy!

"Hi—!" the jumbo gaoler boomed. And through the door he looned, then loomed.

Wyeth wrenched in apprehension.

The gaoler fetched a hefty breath. He flexed his hirsute chest, and biceps.

His hips he slapped. His lips he smacked. The whipped tip of the rope he gripped.

And then the gaoler yanked.

The mummy spun like a humming top. It turned the burning air, a blur. The air it turned it churned, and whirred. Each spin unwound a loop of line that swooshed, unloosed—to hit the ground.

When then the grinning gaoler, snorting, stopped the spinning short.

The bloke broke into focus.

"The farmer!" blurted the banker, blenching.

"It's he!" asserted the woodman, tensely.

"Me it is!" he outburst, densely.

"Busted—!" blustered the lusty gaoler, and thrust the flustered farmer within.

The farmer hobbled past the door.
He wobbled once around the floor.

Then he slowed. His low legs bowed.
Both arms and nether limbs akimboed.

With which he slid, in widdershins.
Then settled down, in sailing tail-spins.

He lay there, grunting bluntly.

"Good grief!" Wyeth cried, flying to
his relief.

The gaoler stooped. The rope he
scooped. He coiled it tight, precise, in loops.

Then, hitching the lot to a glistering
hoop, he scooted off, with a snickery hoot.

The door whammed shut behind him.

The farmer boosted his body up.

"Wyeth—!" He swore. Then kicked the
door. "It's your bum steer's got me in here!"

The farmer soothed his ill-used rear.

"You too . . . are arrested?"

"I'll say!" The farmer brayed.
"All because of your tales!"

"I told no tales!" The woodman wailed.
"I spoke the simple truth!"

"The King says you told tales! So it's
tales you told!"

"Sold!" the banker briskly dittoed.
"So it's tales you told!"

"The King knows I told the truth!"

"Blast—!" The farmer's canines
flashed. "The guard is back! The woods
is ransacked! No trace of a face!"

The farmer paced, then raced, then
paced.

"So it's *me* to take your rap! Up to *me*
to pay your dues!"

Wyeth went sick at the pit of the
stomach.

"Count me too!" The banker beeped,
and tweaked the farmer's teat, discreetly.

The farmer freaked. He snapped
his teeth. He slapped the banker on
either cheek.

"Stop it! Stop it!" Wyeth implored.
"Isn't there trouble enough, and more?"

"Ay!" The flaming farmer roared.
"Nor am I the body to blame!"

"Nor I!" Exclaimed the brainless
banker.

"Nor I!" A shameless voice proclaimed
"The gaoler—!"

"Will you butt out—?" The woodman
shouted. "No one asked your views!"

"Views?" The drooling gaoler cooed.
"I'm here, my dears, with news!"

The farmer stiffened in surprise.

The banker's bloodshot eyes went
wide.

The woodman's face froze in surmise.

"News—!"

"News—!"

"News—?"

"Sure!" enthused the ghoulish gaoler.
"The caper's known! Your scam is blown!
The whole number is come apart!"

The gaoler probed a privy part.

"By noon you'll all be burnt at the
stake! Baked like one big birthday cake!"

He passed, at last, an artful phart.

The farmer choked.

The banker croaked.

The sweat-soaked woodman hung his
head as a pounding sounding at the
outerdoor sent the gaoler bounding off.

CHAPTER
III:III

Anchored by the door, the banker bent an anxious ear to hear.

Through, a slew of voices flew. Too, a giant hullabaloo. Also howls and ghastly growls. Snarls as well, plus nasty yowls.

Then the din commenced to thin. The roar of voices soon surceased. Snarls, then sour growls decreased. Fleeting feet beat out in peace.

The trio waited, breathing bated.

Then the door re-activated.

"The knight—!"

"Good heavens—!"

"It's he—!"

"Quondam knight," he coldly corrected, jawbone boldly projected.

"A con all right!" The gaoler delighted, smiting the knight within.

The knight propelled across the cell. He walked into a wall, and yelled.

His eyes then pied. He
hooked aside. He took a step,
and looked cock-eyed.
    At which his bony body bumped.
And, all angles, down he dumped.
    He lay there, rumbling numbly.
    "Gracious," whispered Wyeth,
hastening to assist him.

    The gaoler rocked. His belly locked.
He sought, then brought out a lollypop.
    Then, popping the lolly betwixt his lips,
he split, while licking his jolly chops.

    The door lammed shut behind him.

Unhorsed, the knight lay stiff as ice is,
mindblown by the swift-grown crisis.
    No dagger dangled at his hip. His mail
was mangled, gauntlets clipped. His rich-
wrought shirt, besmirched with dirt, was
ripped, hung down in dungy strips.
    The knight was quite unsightly.

    "How frightful," murmured Wyeth.
    The knight exploded like dynamite.
    "Then get me out of here!"
    "But how?" the woodman asked,
abashed.
    "By doing what you're told!"

    The knight uprose to half his height,
to tap the text of the tacked-up scroll.
    "Sold!" the banker briskly dittoed.
"Doing what you're told!"
    Wyeth's knuckles whitened.
    "But you're a knight!" he admonished,
astonished. "Plighted to Right!
To Chivalry—! Truth—!"
    The rueful woodman lept aloof.
    "You should be the first to know
there's nothing worse than lying!"
    "Fie!" The knight drew tight his fly.
He pulled a face. Sniffed in distaste.
Plunked a hunk of hair in place.
    With a grim grin he dared declare:
"Times change! Time changes!"
    The cold col of his nose froze.
    "Oh! Sir Esquire—!"
    The banker sucked up to the knight.
"Why—we two—we're soul-mates—!"
    The bucking knight threw up.

    "But," pursued the woodman, con-
fused. "In times like these—why, Right—
why, Truth is wanted most!"
    "Tripe!" returned the burning knight.
"What's wanted is what the King wants!"
    The farmer flailed. A nostril inhaled.
    "And the King wants no tales!"
    "On no account!" The banker quailed.
"Me—! That's why I'm jailed!"

"I told no tales!" Wyeth prevailed.
"I spoke the open truth!"

"Tripe! You must come clean!
Recant—!"

"Recant! Recant!" The
banker panted.

"Recant! Recant!" The
farmer chanted.

"Recant!" The rampant knight
kept ranting.

"Recant? I shan't—! I can't—!
What of —?"

"The face!"

"The scam!"

"The sham!"

"The dream!"

The woodcutter clapped his
ears shut.

"*Will* he recant?" The banker
squirmed.

"He *will* recant?" The farmer
yearned.

"Recant he *will*!" The knight
affirmed.

"Stop it! Stop it! Stop it, the lot of you!"
Wyeth was at his wit's end.

"Quite!" The knight brimmed bright
with spite. "And at this hour the Square
prepares! By noon we'll be but ashes, all!"

The banker bunched up like a ball.

The farmer scrunched against a wall.

"Unless—" piped up the hyped-up
knight. "Unless the woodman confess!"

"Yes!" The tearful banker pressed.
"Wyeth must confess!"

"Yes!" The fearful farmer stressed.
"Wyeth must confess!"

"Yes!" The sneerful knight obsessed.
"The woodman must confess!"

"For, thus the King in his office
advised me! Thus the King in his person
apprised me!"

The choking knight broke out in spots.

"Before he dropped me, then he
popped me, *pat!* into this poxy prison!"

The knight succumbed to sucking his
thumb.

Wrenching, Wyeth clenched a fist.

"Just wait until the Prince hears this!"

"The Prince—?" The farmer blankly
blinked.

"The Prince—?" The knight twice
blinked, then blanked.

"The blinkety-blank Prince—!"

The banker, blaring in despair, cringed
his head in the hinge of an elbow.

"Yes, indeed! Prince Yvian!"

With which the woodman, a mile a
minute, boldly told the princely visit.

"Tripe!" The knight blew up like a kite.
"It's but a dream!" He screamed.

"A dream it is!" The farmer scowled.

He turned green. He looked sick.
He bit his bitten nails to the quick.

"A dream it is!" The banker howled.

He turned red. Tears shed. He bit his bitten lip till it bled.

"It *is* a dream!" The knight yowled.

He turned blue. His hair-do too. He rared to run the woodman through.

"It's not!" shot back the woodman. "Every part is heart-truth! The Prince was here! The face was there! I talked with him! I did!"

His ringing words winged off, unheard.

"Won't any one believe me...?"

But a boom like doom at the outerdoor scotched the gloom of the tomb-like dungeon.

"The guard—!"

The farmer shuddered. His lips stuttered. His knocking knees turned to rubber.

"The guard it is! My number is up—!"

The banker cracked. He reeled back. He started having a heart attack.

"It *is* the guard—!"

The knight looked ill. He lost control. His true blue blood ran chill, then cold.

"Wyeth first!" The banker outburst. "Me—! I am innocent!"

"You're the fat should first to fire!" The farmer spat, then cursed, with ire.

The banker wrinkled in rancour.

"You!" he huffed.

"You!" was puffed.

"You!"

"You!"

"You!"

"You!"

"*Thou—!*"

Wyeth stared, in rare despair.

The knight convulsed, engulfed in revulsion.

At which the door cracked back and hard, and into the cell barged in the guard, wielding shields and lances.

They struck a stance, arms advanced, as by them danced a dashing captain, slashing a flashing sword, and passing.

The banker hid behind the knight who hid behind the stolid farmer who slid behind the solid woodman who held, jelled, to the captain.

"Front and center!" the captain snapped. "The King commands thee to report!"

The woodman's racing heartbeat sped. He braced his legs. Tossed his head.

Fingers crossed, he paced straight forth.

As the captain foined then feinted, the banker, knight and farmer fainted.

"Avaunt—!" The captain lunged, then plunged. "On the short to the court of the King!"

85

CHAPTER
IV

CHAPTER
IV:I

The cold feel of bold steel sent the woodman reeling after the captain.

He, already out the dungeon doors, hustled and rustled and bustled about, running shadows through.

Once beyond the prison precincts the party marched down a high-arched passage, long, and scarved in darkness. Then they coursed a carven cloister. Next was crossed a sort of fore-court.

Ahead, lamps lit up a flight of stairs which spiralled, whitely, out of sight. The captain struck for it.

Again the woodman had the notion unseen eyes screened every motion.

They scaled quickly. The steps swept upwards, steeply slanting, canting right to a rising ramp. Pillars of stone at either side gleamed by greenish torch-beam. A light, at height, flared then faded.

Soon granite gave to fine-grained marble. The air cleared. Damp disappeared. Underfoot, the rough-hewn cobbles turned to burnished flagstones.

When then the captain, cutting a corner, halted within a vaulted chamber, wide, supplied with bona fide sunlight.

Before, there loomed a lofty portal, overhung by a royal device and scutcheon.

"From here," the leering captain sneered. "The King will see you singly!"

The captain clapped.
The guards stepped back.
Wyeth rehearsed the worst.

By the blunt of his blade the captain dealt the door one thump.
Slowly it swung ajar.

As Wyeth went in several things happened at once.

The door, behind his back, snapped shut. A weight, within his chest, oppressed.

And, before his sore-tried eyes, a viscid vapour void of shape, steamed, then seemed to solidify:—and Ulphius urged him forward.

Woozy, the woodman walked towards him.

Fat, the King sat, squat on his throne, perched upon a pyramid of pillows, each one rich, and gorgeously stitched.

His hennaed beard showed fiery red. A crown of white gold glowed on his forehead.

The grid of his brow was furrowed, and deep. Beneath peaked lids, eyes — oblique — peeped.

The King seemed there, yet elsewhere.

The woodman moved to make obeissance.

"Oooh—!" The King out-cried surprise. "*You* need not stand on ceremony!"

He smiled a smile of wide circumference.

Wyeth frowned, toeing the ground.

"Am I not your prisoner?"

"Indeed you were," the King concurred. His legs he crossed. He fussed, then coughed.

"Or, so to say...well still...well, may be..."

Ulphius checked, then looked perplexed.

Disarmed, the woodman turned out his palms.

"So to say?"

"Yea...Yea."

The woodman fetched a breath.

"You tease," he reasoned, evenly. "For, what can a captive ask?"

The King twitched. He fitted together his fingertips.

"In your particular case, my friend... why, almost anything..."

Ulphius winked or barely blinked while Wyeth tried to work it out.

"Very well," said he, at last. "I only ask you free the others. What wrong I may have said or done I alone should atone for."

"That may be," soothed Ulphius, smoothly.

Wyeth gulped. "They'll be released?"

The King threw up his dewy hands.

"Why, it's as good as understood."

The woodman buoyed, then jumped for joy.

"Against..." The King leaned forward, keenly. "Against a s-small...or...paltry... f-fealty."

"A fealty?"

"A favour..."

"A favour?"

"A trifle..."

"A trifle?"

"A pittance..."

"A pittance..."

The King applied his pious eyes.

"A topic of but microscopic importance."

He swivelled about, tugging a tiny table out. Atop, a furled-up parchment lay. As well, a quill and ink-horn.

"But sign your name," sighed he benignly. "All the rest shall follow . . ."

A driblet of spit slipped from a lip.

"But what's the gist of it?" Wyeth enquired.

The King unrolled the scroll as a whole.

"Just have a look and see..."

The woodman shook, but took it.

J. LIKED.

X _____
Wood cutter.

X _____
the King.

91

Wyeth whacked the parchment flat. With a crackling snap it furled it up, whereat the woodman whirled away.

"I can not sign!" cried he.

"Then make your mark," the King quoth, starkly.

"Nor jot nor dot I'll make! Not I!"

"So—? What holds your hand?"

"My heart—!"

The King giggled. His gold buttons jiggled.

"Bravo!" He cheered. Then sneered, and severely.

"But now then, let's get down to business!"

Tittering still, the King collected the scroll, then quill. The text he checked, then flexed his fingers.

Anointing the point in jet-black ink, he set his name down, dexterously.

"Hurry!" urged Ulphius, finishing flourishing. "All cavils and doubts must unravel by noon!"

Eagerly, Ulphius proferred the plume. Woodenly, Wyeth refused it.

Dumbfounded, the King re-extended the pen.

The woodcutter spurned it away once again.

Astounded, Ulphius tendered the quill.

Wyeth re-turned back the quill with a will. . .

Ulphius' face replaced by frowns, he paced the throne, round and around . . .

He jumped, confronting the woodman, bluntly.

"Fool!" He hissed. "Then what do you want? Which your wishes? Quit this d-dawdling, this dickering, now!"

He flung the flat of his fist in a palm.

"Name your terms and price!"

Up went Wyeth's eyebrows.

"Bah!" cried Ulphius. "None is priceless!"

"That's untrue," the woodman said, as steady as he stood there.

"No I say! There's none! Not one!"

"Yes there is! There is some one!"

Burning eyes turned on the woodman.

"Sauce! Giv'st me the lie?"

"Sir, I do not lie."

"Thick in the throat thou liest!"

"A lie, sir, is a lie."

"Snot! Dare to contradict us?"

"I say but what I know, sir."

"Hah! The brag of knowing!"

Thumbs drummed down a coming tantrum.

"Why, I know no more than any knows."

"Rot! What can one know? What maketh knowing?"

"Why, what one has heard and seen one knows."

"Ech! Then what can be heard when the Word is blurred? What can be seen when the seer is screened?"

". . .?"

"Dolt! Can'st tell the madman from his madness? Know the dreamer from his dream—?"

"What's the difference? It's not a dream!"

"What's not? Why not?"

"The face, I mean. It's not! It's not!"

The King looked over, crookedly.

"Nor then the loom your longing stayed for—?"

"No!"

"The spark that you in darkness prayed for—?"

"No! No!"

"A spume your coddled frenzy fashioned—?"

"No! No! No!"

"*Is it a figment of your passion—?*"

Wyeth glanced outrance at Ulphius.

"Such words shame sense! They mock themselves! They spoil right reason of her seasoned fruits, delivering still-born monsters!"

The woodman's tightened body brightened.

"I know! I know! Because . . ."

"Because—?"

"Because . . ."

"Because of what—?"

Wyeth made his mind up.

"Because of the Prince!" cried he, candescent, and pressed his hand to his breathing breast.

"Yvian—!"

The King cringed back. His face went black.

"A plague on the Prince!"

The King's eyes blazed. He looked depraved.

"May nails impale that tell-tale tongue!"

"It's not a tale!" cried Wyeth.

Ulphius' bulging eyeballs rolled. The knolled tip of his thick tongue lolled.

He budged, then bounded so hard by Wyeth their noses nearly nudged.

"Dare swear. . .?"

His nostrils flared. He forced for air.

"Against your life—?"

The woodman swallowed. His chest hollowed.

Still he fought shy of replying.

The King gasped. He grasped at a cushion. Down to the dais he dashed, then slashed it.

"Your *life*, wretch—!"

The woodman winced. He saw an inch of seam unstitched. He picked some sundered threads up.

Mulling a moment, he twirled a wisp at random round his wrist.

"W-Wyeth . . ." was choked, in stammers, in starts.

The woodman tarried, to carry a fallen feather up.

"W-Wyeth . . ." was croaked, in clamours, in parts.

The King convulsed. "Now cease, and sign the scroll!" He screeched.

"I may not, I," sighed Wyeth, softly.

"You can! You will—! You m-must needs sign—!"

The wringing King seized on the quill. He ran to ram it in Wyeth's offending fingers.

The woodman whizzed away.

"I'll not so much as touch it!"

"Take the quill!" Ulphius shrilled.

"I won't!" cried Wyeth.

"You will!" cried Ulphius.

"I won't!" cried Wyeth.

"You will!" cried Ulphius.

"Won't!"

"Will!"

"Won't!"

"Will!"

"No!"

"Yes!"

"No!"

"Yes!"

"No!"

"Maybe—?"

Wyeth nipped nimbly by the King's clutch.

"No!"

"Yes!"

"No."

"Yes!"

"No."

"Yes! Oh, yes—!"

"No."

Ulphius stamped his frantic feet. He champed, then clamped his gold-tamped teeth.

Against his hams his hands he beat. Down he slammed them, each by each.

His eyes, teeth, cheeks, flashed, gnashed, bleached.

"D-dare d-defy us . . .?"

Highly drily Wyeth whispered:

"I do dare . . ."

The King tottered. He teetered, nearly toppling.

Worrying, Wyeth was willing to aid. Then Ulphius posed a palm upon his brow, and seemed so to steady.

For a meagre moment he made a mouth, and rambled, scrambled, about. When then his beard went weird, and eyes, re-vivified, appeared to pop.

Out of control, the King demolished his cherished scroll. He clobbered the quill, which all-but abolished it.

CHAPTER
IV:II

Flinging the scraps to the singing winds, he tore for the throne, groaning and grimacing.

There, he pounced upon the premier pillow, bounced it most savagely down.
He pounded another. Pummelled its brother.
In one fell swoop he knocked the next for a loop.

Unhinged, the King — spitting a scurillous curse, and worse — slithered a fist to the cushion's midst.
With once vicious twist of the wrist he jerked the whole pile of pillows down upon his yerking feet.
He stamped the flimsy stuffs, then tramped. He battered the silks. He tattered the tassels. Their shattered shreds he scattered about.
One foot he hooked to the hem of a cushion, which held it fixed while the tother inflicted in volleying kicks, which split the seams, stitch by stitch, wherewith the case reversed then burst, showering its store of snow-white feathers in streams across his shovelling feet.

He punted, and bunches went whirling in air. Fistfulls he hurled up sent swirls everywhere.
Then, ripping and slashing, he slit them and thrashed them, and bashed out their stuffings, which — rippling on past the throne, the zone — soon drifted to dunes which, uplifting, mushroomed, then monsooned the King upwards in fluxions of feathers, which widened, occulting the crown altogether,

so that where ago there the King had just been, and there where he was was still there to be seen,

still there all there was to be seen at the scene was a dense screen of stuff and a fall-out of fluff crushed to dust in a blizzard of smithereens...

CHAPTER
IV:III

Wyeth looked on tenterhooks. He
craned his neck. He strained his eyes.
He flailed a flurry of feathers aside.

But still the billowing pillows of white
veiled the kinking King from eyesight.

Yet then the hurly-burly ceased, in lieu
of which true peace took place.

Nor stir produced, nor pip, nor peep,
save some scuffs of feathers touching.

Then *lo!* above the settling down there
loomed the outline of a crown.

Tangent to two too screwed eyes a
semblance of a nose arose.

A chin then seemed, with wooly beard.

Then fuzzy face and ears appeared.

Then shoulders shown, and hands,
and feet.

And all at once the King complete,
coated quite in clinging feathers.

His face glowed red. His eyebrows shed.

A tumid tongue hung from his lips, to
which some mammocked plumage clung.

His neck was flecked with fledgy foam.

His hanging chin bumped his
breastbone.

The King he figged his fist and blew,
and looked loathing at Wyeth.

The woodman could but shake his
head. His mouth made words but
nothing said.

Oddly Ulphius ululated. He fetched
a sigh. His face had set.

He let a moan and, Wyeth fancied,
faded with its ghostly going.

The King subsided, feckless, to the
the throne.

On impact the portal was fractured
back by guards galore galloping in.

Packing a pike and spike apiece, and
uttering screeches and war-like expletives,
each dashed direct for Wyeth.

Stiffing his lip, the woodman with-
stood, despite the thicket of bristling
blades which jammed, which crammed
him in.

Behind, lackeys and vassals justled
and skittered, vying vainly to glimpse him.

Then the captain made entry.

He sported a bonnet with a turned-up
brim, an ostrich plume pinned upon it.
A dapper doublet trimmed his shoulders,
with ruffs in points profuse at either sleeve.

Just past the portal he poised, that all
might mark the figure he cut.

Then, swinging his shiny sword and
sharp, he sliced a smart swath throneward,
mincing along in twinkling boots.

"Pray point me," he pleaded with a
puissant pant, bowed so his brow bumped.

For the present tense the King
seemed spent. He slumped, sunk in
junk, enthroned, heedless of his flunky,

prone but keen to get a word in edgewise.

The hackled head and scabrous chin,
gaze glazed and cadaverous skin — the
filthy fettle the King was in sent shivers
of fear down the spines of the throng.

By and bye he budged.

The court calmed down.
The captain cowed.
The hall wholly hushed.

Ulphius pushed to his feet first.

His eyes, narrowed, arrowed at Wyeth,
whose head, above abutting backs, through
shuttling necks, could well be seen.

Too, the woodcutter reckoned the
King, upon whose lips a second seemed
a sigh or inkling in the offing.

Their gazes met

A twinge impinged.
They pulled apart.
Then that was that.

"Take the woodman! B-break him!
Then stake him—!" the King erupted
truculently.

Up catapulted the captain.

Beneath the brim of his bonnet he
grinned, and his jackboots clicked, though
thick in feathers.

CHAPTER
V

CHAPTER
V:I

Since breaking day a sense of violence
had tarred the town towards disarray.

By dawn all souls were up and about.
Nervous shouts jarred house to house.
By sun-up doors and shutters creaked.
Secret eyes peeked out, discretely.

With daylight guards patrolled the
beat, cajoling footsore folk to their feet.
With daybright tourists traipsed the
streets, replete with carts, and carters
shrieking.

Thugs and muggers circulated.
Pimps, pick-pockets operated.
Coppers stopped a peaceful sit-in.
Kids and oddballs got teeth kicked in.

And still the crowds accrued.
Till each last place and breathing space
was packed, with every mobile manjack
making for the Square.

There, a towering scaffold stood.

Built of stout wood, good and tall,
braced by thick-cut beams withal, it rose
before the castle walls, which blazed with
blood-red banners and black brazen
air flapped.
Intent, the court, in robes of state
awaited Ulphius' advent.
Faceless sentries paced the battlements.

Beneath the scaffold workmen toiled,
sweat-soiled in the broiling sun.

Some stacked logs. Other tinder.
Others still packed kindling high, staking
and shaping a massive pyre, which, fired,
would fry the woodman alive.
Pots of hot coals popped close by.

The milling mob, kept collecting,
fulfilled the confines of the Square; and,
spilling from edges of rooftops and ledges,
heaved and seethed, held just in check by
swarms of guards at arms.
The sun swung near its zenith.

CHAPTER
V:II

When then a ghostly post-horn wailed.
A blast of mostly brass assailed.
Fifes piped up, in knife-sharp scales.

The goggling guards, wrought-up,
jerked taut.
The boggling court, caught-up,
stopped short.
Aroused, the crowd let out a shout.
And then a hail, a gale of handclaps
as the castle gates sailed back.

A low blow of whistles echoed.

For, first a band of pock-marked
shock troops goose-stepped out, with
broadswords brandished.

A slow swell of yells crescendoed.
Then a knavish squad of guards waving
staves and spears appeared.

A real squeal of feeling followed.

Last, a picked platoon of dragoons
paraded past in strict formation.

A peal outburst, of adulation.

A hundred hats were flung in air.
Flowers showered everywhere. Cheers to
spare earsplit the Square.
Calm, the men-at-arms marched on;
and then, at whiles, in well-drilled files,
re-deployed in trapezoids roundabout
the scaffold.
Then wheeled, installed in walls of
tall shields.

The crowd, which shifted, now
plunged, now twisted, and all-but blistered
its lungs for whistling.

The guards dug in.
The court grew grim.
The Square prepared for fairly
anything.

A guard grabbed a gone-mad girl,
and hurled her to the ground.

When then ten thousand eyes caught
sight of the farmer, banker, knight!

A din akin to rolling thunder rumbled
through the throng.

For, jabbed, half-dragged into the
Square — in chains — the trio looked
a fright.

At the fore, the farmer swore.
His arms were bruised. Body abused.
Stripped, his back was whipped, contused.
His breaking face was laced with gore.
Sweat outpoured from each poor pore.
Core-sore, the farmer roared.

The yammering mob clamoured for
for more.
And then the Square fell quiet.

Next the knight, who feigned disdain.
Livid his lips. Frigid his mein. Rigid
his torso, and backbone still more so.
His eyeballs burned like urns of flame.
He laughed while biting bits of chain.
The blighted knight seemed quite
insane.
The howling crowd defamed his name.
And then the Square fell quiet.

In tears, the banker brought up the rear.
And grabbed at the chain. And
grabbed, and again. And, fumbling, he
tangled, and, mumbling, he stumbled.
Then fell face down on dung and grit.
Expunging grungy skin from a lip.
The banker bade quits to his wits.

The snickering crowd hooted and
hissed.

The banker frothed at the farmer,
frothed at the banker, back to farmer
back to banker back to farmer who — quick
as a tomcat — knocked the knight flat.
Whereat the cackling crowd cracked up.

A guard slammed the knight's tight
butt, who clambered back to standing up.
Then, looking crook-eyed at the others,
oddly scrambled on.

A crass blast of laughs soon passed.

From hassled at the castle gates, the
three were baffled through the throng;
then, cast against the scaffold's foot,
clapped in shackles, snapped by hooks.

The farmer whimpered.
The knight just simpered.
The pimply banker got limper and
limper.

Which triggered the rabble to giggles
and sniggers.

Just then a clash of cymbals
sounded.
A bash of bellicose bells abounded.
A mass of monstrous gongs
was pounded.
The mob tossed round.
The guard lost ground.
The farmer, banker, knight got
knocked down.

Whereat the castle gates rocked back.

And out the jaunty captain sauntered, with Wyeth at sword-point before him.

The gawking Square first squawked, then stared, for Wyeth the woodman was worsted for wear.

Lashed, his back was welted, and slashed. Bashed, his body was whelked, and gashed.

His head was flecked with ash and mud. He spat out specks of teeth, and hard blood.

Wyeth was woe to behold.

A burst of booes ensued.

The captain sniffed. Miffed, he hissed. He puntoed, passadoed, stoccadoed, with twist.

Then, sticking his blade in the wood-man's spine, he pricked him crisply towards the pack, to which he tipped his dapper cap.

The crowd skipped back before them.

Wyeth was whisked, quick as could be, through the thick of the fickle assembly, into the mickle of picklepussed guards that ringed the scaffold in.

His stopping heart dropped a beat as the farmer, banker, knight popped upright before him.

"Recant!" the hapless banker bleated.

"Recant!" the helpless farmer pleaded.

"Recant!" the hopeless knight entreated.

Each reached out a seeking hand.

Wyeth sighed. He tried replying. But, dry, his vying tongue kept tying.

Whereat the captain, raged, upstaged. Then dealt the woodman a wicked kick, which sent him wobbling, non-stop, up the struts to the scaffold's top.

And there, for one and all to see, the captain clapped an iron ring that snapped about the woodman's neck.

The length of chain he next attached he bolted to the oaken deck.

Whereat in fact the captain quit him.

Wan, bygone, and woe-begone, Wyeth faced the faithless throng, which tapped its heels and squealed and clapped, ecstatic for the mortal act.

And then a pair of trumpets blared. High and thigh-bone flutes fanfared.

A set of kettle-drums declared.

The crowd roared.

The court adored.

The farmer, banker, knight implored.

Then there stood Ulphius, clad in death-black.

Hard-put, the guard but just thrust back the tumbling, jumbling pack.

For sore seconds Ulphius loomed, his
face a paste-board mask of doom.
    The skin was dread white. Flesh flashed
dead light. Eyes, as through two scissored
holes, showed cold, yet red as sizzling coals.
    His wizened lips would issue words
which only Wyeth knew occurred.
    The King was something else.

    Aghast, the crowd gasped out aloud.
    Downcast, the court, hands clasped,
kept cowed.
    The farmer, banker, knight kow-towed.
    And, as the Square fared more and
more scared, silence settled like a shroud.
    As if entranced the King advanced.
    His spinning eyes pinned Wyeth in.
    The pincered woodman squinted back.
    Then winced, convinced the King's
mad eyes were grabbing round him like
a vise.

    Ulphius' eyes were mesmerizing.
    His dupled pupils sized, were sizing.
    To him it seemed some inmost thought
lay prisoned in the woodman's vision.

    Wyeth sensed the center ailing.
    His reeling feelings felt like failing.
    To him it seemed some long-sought
thought lay caught within the King's
grim vision.

    Ulphius' chilling eyes drilled
through him.
    A will was not his own fulfilled him.
    Their looks locked.
    The woodman's shocked mind
stopped.

    His heart sank.
    His brain went blank.
    And as it were the two were one.

    What? was it? Wyeth, writhing,
wondered, *fake—? no, flash—?
no, figment? dream?*

    The knight, the farmer,
banker screamed.
    Wyeth's green resolve dissolved.

    The woodman went to pieces.
    Quite quietly he whispered:
"Yes . . . I lied . . ."

And Wyeth wept, for what it was worth.

    A dead silence broken but by sick,
sodden sobbing set in.

    The crowd stood stunned.
    The court struck dumb.
    The farmer, banker, knight seemed
undone.
    Him, the King was overcome.

    For all, all promise-informed things
were stripped, ripped-off of promising.
    Hope, all hope for things that are,
had cancelled like a falling star.

    Ghost was gone.
    All ached of fake.
    Nothing was but cheat and hate.
    The world was merely maculate.

Down came all with Wyeth's downfall.

CHAPTER
V:III

Bedlam burst out.
Oaths exploded.
Fists flew.
Two feuding factions squared off for action.
A roar uprose as, hard before the castle doors, a brawl outbroke, a free-for-all.
When one went sprawling, head and heels, blood flooding across his face.

As whistles blew and the guard fell to, the craven captain, blue with fear, raced to the far rear, and safety.
Havened behind his guards' broad backs, he rattled commands then countermands, and stood by should a battle be.
The fighting only heightened.

The captain's eyes slimmed down to slits. He tried to grit his teeth, which clicked.
He yearned to learn the will of the King who, still standing stark as death, gazed, glass-eyed, on what was Wyeth.

When then a banner fluttered down, blackly, to the battleground.

With a pure purr of satisfaction the captain cracked into action.

Burying his blade in the tinder nearby, he kindled a flame he hoisted aloft.

He fanned the blaze with crazy waves.

With waves were crazed he fanned the blaze.

And then he snapped his wrist, then slashed, casting the crackling kindling off.

It spun across, an airborne torch, that dropped atop the timbers stacked beneath the woodman's scaffold.

The tinder took.

A fume, a plume of smoke broke skywards.

Pandemonium proceeded.

A martial mob, now up in arms, charged the guards, agog, en masse.

Enraged, the charged-on guards engaged.

Engaged, the mob charged on, outraged.

Quarters closed.

Limbs locked.

Shock succeeded sudden shock.

When then a storm of thrown stones struck.

Like buckshot brickbats raked the ranks.

A rain of rocks knocked flat a flank.

A guard, then some, stunned by the brunt, grudgingly gave ground.

Frightened from his manic wits, the frantic captain panicked.

Ducking down, he jittered around,

scuttling hither, thither and yon, searching a gap in a tranquil flank.

Then there was one.

The captain dodged. He bobbed and weaved. Streaking forward, he picked up speed.

Like a shot he rocketed through.

Flashing toward the castle gates, hurdling heaps of severed pates, the captain cast his sword away, though fleet afoot, to flee the faster.

The gates clapped shut behind him.

At which a fist of flame uplifted. Smoke, in wispy drifts, outbroke.

Whereat the struts that stayed the scaffold swayed, ablaze—then caved away—

And Wyeth was cut off.

The woodman lept erect.

Choked by swirls of whirling smoke, he wrenched and kicked the chain, the bolt.

In vain. Both bolt and chain retained.

Made to think, and thinking fast, the woodman bent a bight of chain tight about his straining shoulder.

He braced upon a shaky knee. Intense, he tensed his coiled-up body.

He breathed a brief but deep-felt prayer.

Then cannonballed into mid-air.

The links payed out like lightening, outright.

And all at once—brought up taut by Wyeth's weight—the bolt, it budged, then jolted loose!

Planking yanked off with the lot.

Wyeth, like a sack of rocks, went toppling over, rolled, skid flat.

And inches, if that, off the edge slid scraping to a stop.

Blood-red, a star bloomed from his forehead.

Whereat he blacked out.

And, out of time, out of mind, his brilliant body magnified toward one divide of light.

His skeleton snapped him back.

His lungs stung. His ears were ringing. Zeroes in his skull zinged through him.

A hail of voices wailed down spaces. Failing faces sailed away.

He let it, let them be.

A breeze then broke the frieze of smoke. And in a flash all froze to focus.

He took one look.

One good look he took.

One good look was all he took.

All it took was one good look.

For, gone, he knew, was chaste good grace. Gone for good from his embrace.

Gone beyond the world's flung face. Chased, disgraced, to alien spaces.

He forsook for good such graces.

A shout of welcome smote the welkin as, framed in flame, the woodman appeared.

The crowd cheered loud and clear for Wyeth.

The woodman drooped. His eyes he dropped.

Scores of plying arms implored him.

He hung his head. He flinched away.

A host of swaying hands craved towards him.

Quavering, Wyeth wavered back.

Then thrust aside, to hide his black face.

Behind a billowing pillar of smoke, the woodman shrank, which cloaked him blank.

Whereat there was a clap of thunder.

The earth itself seemed smacked asunder.

Splitting timbers spit and rumbled.

A claw of snapping sparks snatched up.

The scaffold sought to step, to stumble.

It lurched, crumbled, then collapsed.

Wrapped in a winding sheet of flame, Wyeth was wasted.

Chaos cut loose.

A surging mob converged on the guard, now left to fight as best it might.

Blade bit blade.

Club hit club.

Slugged bodies thudded into mud.

From gashed flesh gushed ooze and guts. The streets ran red with pools of bloodshed.

When then there came a rain of flame.

A hundred hands flung firebrands.

Numbers more slung blazing bolts.

And countless pails of white-hot nails assailed like meteors hailing down.

Barraged, bombarded, jumped then thumped, the guard faltered, falling back.

At which a weakened flank was breached.

And through the roaring rabble poured, by twos, by fours, then tens then scores.

The guard was good and got at.

Yet, overmatched, it stood and fought, fending endless onslaughts off.

Until a crack platoon packed up.

Battered back by a brute attack, in consternation, it broke formation.

Bunches bled, and fell down dead.

Batches fled, and lost their heads.

Turncoats throat-cut former fellows, to wrest their weapons from them.

The guard was left with no resort.

Forced, it beat a bitter retreat, battling to reach the castle.

Where, snug in a plugged-up bastion above, the ex-captain, upped to major, masterminded defence.

He checked his text on tactics.

Whereat a vat of boiling oil, overthrown from the castle walls, doused the guard in fireballs.

And jagged bits and blocks and rocks scattered flying flak and shrapnel.

Worse, the major's men-at-arms commenced firing, fired at will, aimed true, and shot to kill.

In shock the guard rocked back.

Cauldrons full of molten lead then splattered on their melting heads.

Screaming guards dissolved in steam.

And then the mob was on them.

Sticks, steel, knees, knives maimed, mayhemmed, claimed lives.

At bay, in disarray, the guard, betrayed, was slaughtered to a man.

Somehow spared despite the strife,
the banker, farmer and the knight—
linked for life, run mad with fright—
fought to flee in three directions.

The knight lashed left with all his might.
The thrashing farmer backlashed right.
Betwixt, the banker bashed and
kicked. And flopped, and flip-flopped,
twisting over.

The knight cursed out the farmer cursed
the banker cursed the farmer back to
banker back to farmer back to knight.

Who, eyes like deadlights, drew a knife.
And sliced the banker twice in two.
And slew the luckless farmer too.
The pair stared. Their sad eyes stopped.
They dropped dead on the spot.
Two lightless souls took flight.

Sweat swept off the knight's wrecked
face flesh.

He raised his blood-bathed blade
afresh.

Then, crying mercy for his life, the
brainsick knight sheathed the knife
precisely in his whistling windpipe.

Sunlight jigged off red wet metal.
The knight rose, stiff to his toes.
He babbled one last scarlet breath.

Then crashed flat, tapped by death.

A spectral being startled seeing.
"The forest is on fire!"
Like nightmare, fear flared through
the Square.

At a burst the throng dispersed.
Berserk, a reckless horde disgorged
down the spoking, smoking sideroads,
in through splintered doors and out,
smashing what got in its getaway.
A beggar beat a blind man dead.
A burgher choked the bloke ahead.
A legless laggard's throat was slit.
His purse was snatched, two coppers in it.
Riff-raff fell to pilling and pelling, and
felling the helpless and lame.

Then, run amok, the rioting ruck
havocked through the high- and by-ways,
taking, breaking what goods it could,
screaming obscenely between them.
A priest committed suicide.
A prophet burned himself alive.
A bishop brained a crippled dame.
He climaxed in her corpse, in flames.
Gangs of syphilitic rats, scuttling up
from scum-packed sewers, fanged to bits
her hot cadaver.

Walking wounded went insane.

Fighting tykes puled in pain.

Crying, lying dying prayed.

Windy footfalls fled away.

Serene, the King surveyed the scene.

A bitter sun was spitting on a silent
waste of blood-soaked rubble.
In ruins, the Square was strewn
with junk.
The blasted streets seemed one
vast dump.
A reeking haze seeped from a mash
of blazing trash and pissed-out ash.

Corpses littered limp as lumps.
Butchered bodies lay in chunks.
Hacked-off stumps from human
trunks, stiff with gore, were going black.

Far off, the conflagration spread.
The forest flamed and flamed, blood-red.
        No tree was spared; nor shrub; nor leaf.
Devastate that wasted heath.
        Then salt was sown into the earth.
Then came rain, a muddy curse.
        The countryside was gutted, flat.
No leaf of life took after that.

        The King burst out in squeals of
laughter.
        He lived to rule forever
after.

THE END

Concluded January 1977, Sausalito, California.